For Big T and Baby R — and their penguins, too. — A.S

For my family. — A.A

First published 2022 by Macmillan Children's Books
an imprint of Pan Macmillan
The Smithson, 6 Briset Street, London EC1M 5NR
EU representative: Macmillan Publishers Ireland Ltd, 1st Floor,
The Liffey Trust Centre, 117–126 Sheriff Street Upper,
Dublin 1, D01 YC43
Associated companies throughout the world.
www.panmacmillan.com

ISBN 978-1-0350-2396-7

Text copyright © Andrew Sanders 2022
Illustrations copyright © Aysha Awwad 2022

1 3 5 7 9 8 6 4 2

A CIP catalogue record for this book is available from the British Library.

Printed in China

FSC
www.fsc.org
MIX
Paper | Supporting
responsible forestry
FSC® C116313

Andrew Sanders Aysha Awwad

WHERE HAS ALL THE CAKE GONE?

MACMILLAN CHILDREN'S BOOKS

Albert! Where has all the cake gone?

I don't know.

Did you eat the cake?

I did not eat the cake.

Are you *sure* you did not eat the cake?

Yes.

Really?

It could not have been me.
I was in the kitchen.

Aha! That is where
the cake was.

Yes. I was in the kitchen,
when the penguins got me.

The penguins?

Yes. And they put me in a large jar of marmalade.

Penguins?

Yes. And then they took
me to the train station.

Penguins?

Yes. And they took
me to France.

In a jar of marmalade?

No. In a train.

Oh, wait. Yes. I was still in the jar of marmalade too.

Penguins took you to France?

Eventually. We got a bit lost first.

And then what happened?

They took me up a mountain.

That sounds quite unbelievable.

I know. I was surprised that penguins could climb mountains, too.

Which mountain was it?

A big white one.
It had kangaroos on it.

I don't think this is true, Albert.
Kangaroos do not live on French mountaintops.

These ones were on holiday.

Kangaroos on holiday?

Yes. And we all went skiing.

With kangaroos?

No. With skis.

Oh, wait. Yes.
With the kangaroos, too.

Chez
Roo

You went skiing with
kangaroos and penguins?

Yes. And then we
all built snowmen.

How many snowmen
did you build?

Four hundred and twelve.

That sounds like a lot.

And then we had
a snowball fight.

With the snowmen?

Don't be silly.
Snowmen can't move.

The kangaroos and the penguins
had a snowball fight?

Yes. And the kangaroos were winning.

Really?

Until I got out of the marmalade and managed to roll one big snowball down a hill.

Really?

Yes. And it knocked all of the kangaroos off into the sunset, and the penguins won.

Are you sure this is all true, Albert?

Yes.

Then why are you covered in pieces of cake?

Well, when the penguins brought me home,
they decided to eat some cake to celebrate.

So, you didn't eat any of it?

No. In fact, I tried to stop the penguins from eating the cake, too. But it got quite messy.

Really?

Yes. That's why I'm covered in cake.

But you're sure you didn't eat any of the cake?

Very sure.

Not one piece?

Not one piece.

These penguins sound very naughty. I wish they had not eaten my cake.

Me too. I did tell them off for you.

You did?

I huffed a lot and then I told them that I wasn't too angry with them. I was just disappointed.

That is how I feel, too.
I suppose I will just have
to make another cake.

Yes. But don't worry,
I will help you.

Thank you.

You're welcome.

And I guess we will just have to keep it away from the naughty penguins this time, Albert.

I guess we will.

Shoo.